We're Going on a Trip

Christine Loomis
illustrated by Maxie Chambliss

Morrow Junior Books New York

Watercolors were used for the full-color artwork.
The text type is 14-point Century Book.

Text © 1994 by Christine Loomis. Illustrations © 1994 by Maxie Chambliss.

1 2 3 4 5 6 7 8 9 10

Library of Congress Cataloging-in-Publication Data
Loomis, Christine. We're going on a trip / Christine Loomis; illustrated by Maxie Chambliss.   p.   cm.
Summary: After traveling by plane, train, and car, three families reach their vacation destinations.
ISBN 0-688-10172-0 (trade).—ISBN 0-688-10173-9 (lib. bdg.)
[1. Travel—Fiction.   2. Vacations—Fiction.]   I. Chambliss, Maxie, ill.   II. Title   PZ7.L874We
1994   [E]—dc20   93-17592   CIP   AC

Note to Parents

Traveling together as a family can be a rewarding experience. Without the pressures of work, school, and household tasks to interfere with your time together, you can relax and enjoy one another's company.

Traveling with children can also be a trying experience. Whining, squabbling, boredom, overtiredness, and hunger can turn a family trip into an ordeal. Fortunately, there are things parents can do to avoid the pitfalls. By planning wisely and giving your children reassuring information, you can solve many problems before they arise and make your family vacation a time everyone will look forward to—and remember—with happiness.

PLANNING

When you travel with children, planning is paramount—and children *should* be part of the planning process. One way to involve them is to let them help with the itinerary. Let the kids choose if you should go to the science museum or the aquarium first. Giving kids a say in the itinerary will help them feel it's *their* vacation too.

Once you know where you're going, talk to the children about what to expect. The idea of sleeping away from home can be unsettling for many kids. Let them know they can bring a favorite toy and that you will be nearby. Emphasize that they will be doing many of the same things they do at

home. They can still read a book before bedtime no matter where the bed is. They can still look at the same stars and sing the same songs, but they'll also get to do some new and exciting things, too.

Also explain exactly where you will be going. If you're going to a hotel or motel, explain what that will be like. If you're going to Grandma's house, you can tell your children stories about when you were growing up with Grandma. You don't have to overload them with information, just give them enough so that they have something concrete to relate to. Remember, this is a new experience for them.

PACKING

Everyone should pack lightly. This isn't easy, but the key is to be realistic. Children never wear all of the clothes parents pack for them. If you bring along a bottle of hand-washing detergent, you can give clothes a quick wash and hang them to dry while you're out sight-seeing.

Kids can help with packing, too. Small children can gather the special things for the bag they will keep with them in the car or on an airplane. Older kids can pack for themselves. Check to see that they include essentials, such as underwear and a toothbrush.

Leave out comfortable easy-on, easy-off clothes for traveling. Dressing kids in layers they can take off or add to depending on the temperature makes everyone happier.

AT YOUR DESTINATION

Once you've arrived, keep in mind you're on vacation. Plan plenty of free time. A vacation in which every moment is filled with something to do can make everyone cranky.

It's also important to plan time for naps, snacks, and regular meals. While kids like excitement, they need routines and rituals in order to feel secure. Sticking to regular schedules and routines with regard to eating and sleeping can eliminate the crankiness that results from hunger or lack of sleep.

Schedule activities according to the abilities and needs of your youngest family member. That may seem unfair to older children, but the fact is if the youngest can't keep up, it will not be a fun time for anyone. Sometimes dividing up the family can solve conflicts. If older children want to do something the youngest can't, arrange for a sitter for the youngest or divide kids between parents. The same is true of activities for younger kids that may bore older siblings.

Don't forget to schedule some adult-only time. Parents need a vacation, too. You can go out to dinner or to that museum the kids won't like. If you're visiting relatives who live far away from you, they will probably like the chance to spend time alone with your children, developing their own special relationship. If you're staying in a hotel or resort, it may have a supervised children's program. The kids will meet other kids and have an opportunity to do things they might not do otherwise.

Even if there is no organized program, arrange for a sitter. Many hotels have off-duty staff who baby-sit, or the hotel may provide a list of local, reliable agencies. (If hotel staff is available, ask the concierge for a sitter who has been with the hotel for a while and who has proved popular with other parents; if agencies are recommended, make sure sitters are bonded and that there have been no complaints. Give sitters specific, detailed instructions about food, bedtimes, routines, TV, discipline, etc. Since you don't know this sitter and he or she doesn't know your family, you have to spell things out even more clearly than you would with your sitter at home.) Leaving kids with a sitter doesn't mean you're leaving them to be bored or unhappy. Depending on the ages and interests of your children, sitters can take them for walks, to the pool or game room, or out to eat. Kids consider it a treat to have room service, so you can also arrange for them to order in. And most hotels have VCRs and tapes for families to use, or free cable, or pay TV. Arrange your outing for a time when a favorite children's movie is on.

TRAVELING BY CAR

When you're packing for a road trip, include travel games, soft toys, washable markers, peel-off-sticker books, paper, and crayons. A tape player with headphones is also a good choice. And don't forget a small blanket for sleeping, even in the summer, and small pillows (camping pillows are the perfect size).

Pack snacks that won't crumble or leak. If you have room, a small cooler on the floor in the back allows kids to get their own snacks.

The best part about car travel is that getting there is part of the vacation, which means you shouldn't try to set records reaching your destination. Stop to take pictures, to look at local sites, to buy post-cards for a trip album. The American Academy of Pediatrics suggests parents stop about every two hours to let children stretch and run around.

The best time to travel varies from family to family. Some like getting up early, driving, then stopping in time to use the motel pool. That gives children something to look forward to at the end of a long drive. Other parents like doing some driving when children are likely to sleep. Whatever works for you is fine—as long as the total time in the car each day is not more than about eight hours.

Give children information in ways that they can understand. For example, telling them that you will arrive at the hotel at dinnertime will mean more to them than hearing that it is a seven-hour drive. Remember, too, that children take things very literally. An offhand remark such as "We'll be sleeping on the road tonight" may have kids imagining all sorts of scary things.

Territorial disputes are, of course, one of the biggest hazards of family car travel. "He's on my side" is a complaint parents hear frequently, along with "She's making noise" and the dreaded "She looked at me." Keeping kids from being bored is one way to eliminate petty squabbles, so when arguments begin, take out the games and activities. Many parents keep a bag of goodies in the car, doling out new ones as the miles pass. Changing seats may also help. One parent can occasionally take the backseat and give special time to one child while the other child becomes "navigator" in the front seat, reading maps, checking routes, and counting off the miles.

Whatever is going on in the car, keeping your children in a safety seat or seat belt is the most important thing you can do. Automobile accidents are the primary cause of death and disability for children under age four; they account for almost 25 percent of all accidental deaths of children aged one to fourteen. Buckling up should not be negotiable. Do your kids a favor by setting an example; always wear your seat belt in the car.

IN AN AIRPLANE

Whether you fly at night when little ones are sleeping or during the day when they may be most cooperative and even-tempered depends on your children. Keep their personalities in mind when you book flights.

Remember to order children's meals when you book your flights, but keep in mind that planes—and therefore meals—are often delayed. *Always* pack snacks in your carry-on bag, including something to drink. If you're traveling with an infant or toddler, include a bottle of water for mixing with juice or formula. Airplane water is treated with chemicals and can upset young children's sensitive stomachs.

Your carry-on bags should always include a change of clothes for each family member and a swimsuit (if your destination includes swimming). Luggage, too, can be delayed. And don't count on finding formula or diapers at airports in case of problems. Pack enough baby supplies to last the whole day, even if you're only on a two-hour flight.

If your child has never been on an airplane before, don't wait until you're at the airport to talk about what it will be like. A good time frame for a young child is two or three days before a trip. If he has questions or fears, you'll be able to deal with them before the vacation. Again, reassure your child about the things that matter most to him. Let him know that you'll be there, that (at least some of) his most cherished possessions can go with him, and that he will be able to have juice and a snack if he wants it. If you're enthusiastic and positive, your child will probably adopt the same attitude.

Don't forget to give your child some idea of what takeoff and landing will be like. Because of the noise, the sudden acceleration or braking, and the possibility of uncomfortable ear pressure, takeoff and landing can be the most problematic for inexperienced flyers. Giving kids something to drink—a bottle for babies and juice with a straw for older children—can help relieve ear pressure. A hand to hold, a smile, and some concrete information should reassure children about the rest.

Mention that flight attendants are going to talk about safety, too. This is especially important for children old enough to understand the information. Discussion of emergencies can be frightening unless children know that this is standard procedure and that airlines are simply taking the same kinds of precautions parents take around the house, in the family car, at the beach, etc.

You might also want to mention airplane lavatories. Adults sometimes forget that something so commonplace can be scary to small children. The sound of an airplane toilet flushing is loud—and very different from the sound a home toilet makes. If your child is frightened of loud noises or toilets—and many children are—let him leave the lavatory before you push the button.

Also important for young children on an airplane is the use of a safety seat. Many experts recommend the use of safety seats on airplanes for infants and toddlers—and not just for takeoff and landing. It has become clear that even during periods of turbulence unrestrained babies are at risk of injury and death.

If you have a child under two years of age, put him in an approved car seat for the flight (seats made in recent years have a sticker stating that they are approved for use on aircraft). When you make your reservations, let the airline know you plan to bring a car seat on board. If the airline doesn't allow this, make reservations with an airline that does. In addition, make sure all of your children have seat belts loosely fastened around them whenever they're in their seats. That goes for parents, too.

ON A TRAIN

The great thing about train travel is that it gives children a chance to walk around and to look at endlessly changing—and therefore interesting—scenery.

Taking a train, however, does take longer than flying, and it's best to consider time on the train as part of your vacation rather than just a means of getting to a destination. Enjoy the chance to play games, read together, or just talk. Use the time to get out the brochures and plan your vacation itinerary or read further about the sites you will see. When you tire of all that, give the kids Colorforms or peel-off stickers; train windows make an excellent "storyboard."

One caveat is that train snack bar and restaurant totals can run high. You're wise to pack your own snacks and drinks if you want to keep costs down.

However you travel, wherever you go, plan to have fun. Read books together, play games you haven't played since you were a child traveling with your own parents, or just sit around talking. Spending time together without commitments and distractions is a luxury for families in today's busy world, so take advantage of it. That's what family vacations are all about.

Are you going on vacation?
Vacations are fun!

When you go on vacation, you leave home for a little while to see new places and meet new people. Or maybe to see someone you know who lives far away. You might even make a new friend. Then, after a while, you'll always come home again.

There are lots of ways to travel on vacation.
You can drive in a car.
Or fly in an airplane.
Some people like to ride on trains.

How are you going to travel?
Who are you going to see?

In an Airplane

Julius and his mom are flying on an airplane to visit
Grandma. Julius's dad has to stay home and work, so
Julius promises to tell him everything about the trip.

Julius waves good-bye. His dad blows him a kiss. "That
kiss is good for one week," he calls to Julius. "Then you
have to come home for a new one."

On the way to the airport, Julius holds his lion very close. "Mama," he says, "I think Caspar is a little nervous about flying."

"Oh, I think Caspar will like flying. Does he like to look out the window?"

"I think so," Julius says.

"Would he feel better if he could meet the pilot?"

"I'm pretty sure he'd feel better then," Julius says.

At the airport, there are lots of long counters. People in neat uniforms stand behind them.

A ticket agent takes Julius's green suitcase. It will go in a compartment in the bottom of the airplane. The lady puts special tags on the suitcase so it will go on the same plane as Julius.

"You're all set." She smiles. "Your plane is at Gate Two."

On the way to the gate, Julius and his mom have to stop at security. Everything they're carrying has to be x-rayed to make sure it's safe to take on the airplane.

Julius watches the monitor. He sees all the shapes of things inside his backpack. "Hey, this is a funny TV," he calls out. Then a familiar shape appears. "Look, Mama, it's Caspar!"

When Caspar comes down the ramp, Julius gives him a big hug. "You did great on TV," Julius says.

At Gate 2, a gate agent checks their tickets; then Julius and his mom can go on board.

Inside the plane, a flight attendant helps Julius and his mom find their seats. There are rows and rows of seats. Julius thinks it looks kind of like a movie theater.

The airplane has a kitchen, which is called a galley. All of the food is delivered in refrigerated trucks. The flight attendants check to see that they have everything they need before they leave.

Julius and Caspar visit the cockpit, where the captain and copilot sit. The cockpit is a tiny room with a windshield for the pilot to look out of, and hundreds of buttons and switches and dials. There's even a computer.

Julius wonders how the captain knows which buttons to push.

"You have to go to a special school to learn how to be a pilot," the captain tells Julius.

"Maybe I can be a pilot when I grow up."

It's almost time to take off. Mama fastens her seat belt. "You see that flashing sign up there, Julius? That means the captain wants everyone to buckle up now."

Julius does. Then he squirms around some. But after a while, he forgets that the seat belt is even there.

Julius and Caspar look out the window. The airport
is a busy place. Airplanes are taking off and landing.
Luggage goes back and forth on big carts, and people
stand on the ground helping the pilots park the airplanes.

In a few minutes, Julius feels the airplane start to
move. Then it goes faster. And the engines get louder.
Julius gets a funny feeling in his stomach and his ears.

He yawns to make his ears feel better, and when he looks
out the window again, they are up in the air.

"Look," Julius whispers to Caspar. "The airport got smaller."

It's been two hours since Julius left home. He's ready for *another* breakfast on the plane.

Afterward, Julius and Caspar look at the clouds. "Hey, look at that," Julius says to Caspar. "The clouds are down instead of up!"

The captain's voice comes over the loudspeaker. He tells Julius and the other passengers that the airplane is 32,000 feet in the air and flying more than five hundred miles per hour.

No wonder Julius has to fly for only two and a half hours to see Grandma. If he and his mom were driving in a car, they wouldn't get to Grandma's house until tomorrow.

Julius looks out the window again. He can see a town getting closer and closer as the airplane flies lower and lower. Then Julius hears a noise underneath him. "Did you hear that, Caspar? Mama says the landing wheels are coming down."

With a bump, the airplane is on the ground, zooming down the runway. Then there's another loud noise. "Mama says that's the captain putting on the brakes," Julius tells Caspar. "Don't worry.

"Good-bye, airplane," Julius calls as he follows the other passengers out of the plane and into the terminal, where they will pick up their luggage.

Someone calls to Julius. It's Grandma!

Grandma is having a family reunion. At Grandma's
house, Julius meets Uncle Bill and Aunt Irene. He meets
Olivia and Theo, too. "These are your cousins, Julius."
Julius and Theo look at each other. "Hey," they say to
Grandma. "He looks just like me!"

Julius's aunts and uncles and cousins have come from all over for the reunion.

"We came on a train," Olivia tells Julius. "We rode all night."

"What was a train like?" Julius wants to know.

"We ate dinner in the dining car, with white tablecloths and matching napkins," Olivia tells him. "And the water jumped around in the glasses like waves at the beach. Then Theo and I walked through six cars and back again, but every one looked the same. When it got dark, Mama and Daddy and Theo fell asleep. But I stayed awake and watched the moon. Everywhere we went, the moon followed right along."

At the end of the week, it's time to fly back home. "Caspar likes flying now," Julius tells Grandma.

Julius is sad to say good-bye, but he's excited, too. He can't wait to get back home and tell Daddy all about his trip. He has a lot to tell.

You'll have a lot to tell about your vacation, too.

In a Car

Ginger and Harry are going on vacation. They're driving to a hotel where they will stay for a few days.

A hotel is a place where lots of families can stay at the same time. A hotel has bedrooms and bathrooms and restaurants.

Mr. Evans is busy packing the car for the trip. There are too many suitcases to fit in the trunk!

When everything is packed, Ginger and Harry scramble into the backseat.

Ginger looks out the window and watches the familiar sights of her town go by. She sees her favorite tree, her nursery school, her best friend's house, and Pepe's Pizza Parlor.

After a while, Ginger doesn't recognize any of the sights. Everything is new and exciting.

"Let's play 'I Spy,'" Harry says. "I'll look out the window and say, 'I spy something red,' and then you have to guess what it is. It won't always be red, though. Ready?"

Ginger nods.

"I spy something green," says Harry.

Ginger looks out the window. "That big green sign," she shouts.

"Right," Harry says. "Now you pick one."

Ginger spies something yellow. Can you guess what it is?

There are lots of interesting things to see when you're traveling in a car. Ginger and Harry stop at a place called a "scenic overlook." That means it's a good place to take a picture.

Harry takes a picture of everyone saying "Cheese."

"We're almost halfway there," says Mrs. Evans. "We can stop for lunch."

Chicken and lemonade taste extragood outside on a sunny day. Harry eats three helpings. He says vacations make him hungry.

Back on the road, Harry listens to the tape player and
Ginger counts the animals she sees. Three cows, four
horses, two gray cats, one dog with spots and one without,
six sheep in a field, and five geese high in the sky.

You can count when you travel, too. You might
count brown barns or white cars or license plates from
Louisiana. At night, you can count lampposts with lights
that aren't lit. You can count almost anything.

After counting, Ginger closes her eyes. When she opens them again, they're at the hotel.

A bellhop in a uniform comes out to get their luggage. He piles it all on a shiny cart and takes it inside.

This hotel is big. It has over four hundred rooms.

Harry and Ginger look around their room. It has two beds, a closet, a TV, a large dresser, a table and chairs, and a bathroom. There's a door that opens right into their mom and dad's room. "We'll leave the door open," Mrs. Evans tells Ginger. "That way, we can hear you if you call us."

There's a lot to do on vacation. Harry and Ginger go to the Dinosaur Museum, and to a museum with lots of paintings.

They also ride on a green bus and visit the zoo. Harry takes more pictures there. He takes pictures of buildings and animals and people. Ginger tries to open her mouth as wide as a hippopotamus's. Harry takes a picture of that!

After a day of sight-seeing, it's nice to sit in the lobby restaurant and get a cool drink. The restaurant is surrounded by potted palm trees and Ginger pretends she's in the jungle.

A girl at the next table smiles. Ginger waves to her. Soon they're both pretending they're in the jungle.

At a hotel, you can meet people from all over the country, or even all over the world. Jeanmarie is visiting from Brooklyn, and Micky is from Bangor, Maine. Charlotte and Angelica have come all the way from Italy. It's fun to make new friends. They'll like meeting you, too.

Soon it's time to leave. All of the luggage goes back on
the shiny cart. Ginger carries her own bag. It's filled with
souvenirs to remind her of her trip: a T-shirt from the
zoo, a miniature dinosaur, and a stack of postcards,
including one of the hotel. Ginger can see the window
of her room in the picture.

Ginger watches the familiar sights of the city go by her car window. She sees the green buses, the entrance to the zoo, and just over the hill, she sees the Dinosaur Museum.

"Good-bye, city. Good-bye, vacation," Ginger calls. "I had the best time ever. I can't wait for vacation next year!"